HELLHOUNDS

BOOKS BY DAVID SANDNER

Fiction
Mingus Fingers

Non-fiction
*The Fantastic Sublime: Romanticism and
Transcendence in Nineteenth-century
Children's Fantasy Literature*
*Critical Discourses of the Fantastic,
1712-1831*

As Editor
Fantastic Literature: A Critical Reader
The Treasury of the Fantastic
(co-edited with Jacob Weisman)
Philip K. Dick: Essays of the Here and Now

BOOKS BY JACOB WEISMAN

Fiction
Mingus Fingers

As Editor
The Sword & Sorcery Anthology
(co-edited with David G. Hartwell)
The Treasury of the Fantastic
(co-edited with David Sandner)
*Invaders: 22 Stories From the Outer
Limits of Literature*
The New Voices of Fantasy
(co-edited with Peter S, Beagle)
The Unicorn Anthology
(co-edited with Peter S, Beagle)
The New Voices of Science Fiction
(co-edited with Hannu Rajaniemi)

HELLHOUNDS

DAVID
SANDNER
& JACOB
WEISMAN

FAIRWOOD PRESS
Bonney Lake, WA

HELLHOUNDS
A Fairwood Press Book
Copyright © 2022
by David Sandner & Jacob Weisman

Fairwood Press
21528 104th Street Ct E
Bonney Lake WA 98391

See all our titles at:
www.fairwoodpress.com

ISBN: 978-1-958880-02-9

Fairwood Press First Edition:
November 2022
Also available in ebook

Cover image © Tom Canty
Cover and book design by Patrick Swenson

Printed in the United States of America

I got to keep movin'
Blues fallin' down like hail
—Robert Johnson
Hellhounds On My Trail

To Leadbelly, Muddy Waters, Lightning
Hopkins, and Mississippi Fred McDowell,
and to Alan Lomax and Chris Strachwitz,
two promethean record producers whose field
recordings helped preserve their legacies for
future generations.

WHEN PEOPLE TALK ABOUT my brother it's as if he was born with the knowledge of cabalism and eschatology. They believe all that crap he spouts in his songs about not being from this planet, how he arrived here as a traveler from a distant galaxy, a black man sent to return his people to their native land.

One of my first memories is of Kenny's birth. Mom and Dad lived in a hovel by the train tracks in Louisiana. I remember women yelling, the windows steamed from water boiling, and the train's low whistle screaming as it hurtled past. He certainly didn't mention being from the Oort Cloud then, or of taking us up to the space station orbiting Jupiter to rendezvous with the mothership. He was like any other newborn kid. He was tiny, no more than six pounds, with a red, angry face squashed like a football.

When I first realized that Kenny was special, truly special, was the summer of 1960, right after my junior year in high school, my last year in school. By then, Mom had sent Kenny and me to live in California with Aunt Lydia for a while. It was the summer I formed my first band and played real gigs around town. It was also the summer I almost lost my brother.

K ENNY SHOOK MY SHOULDER AGAIN. I pulled the bed sheet to my chin and turned to face the mattress. I knew I should get up and see what he wanted. But I just wanted to sleep a little longer through the hot afternoon. I had been dreaming of a cool fog off the San Francisco Bay.

"Go away, Kenny." My voice sounded throaty, like it wasn't mine. I tried to clear it.

Kenny shook me again. He said nothing. He didn't like to talk much.

"What?" I said, loudly. But he had won already, and I pushed myself out of the bed to stand unsteadily in the unfamiliar, dark wood-paneled spare bedroom of my Aunt's house. I pushed Kenny, but not hard.

I parted the white, frilled curtains and looked out the window.

At first I didn't see anything but the old road disappearing over the rise, lined by scrub and sand. Nobody there. I was about to pound Kenny. Then I saw a dust cloud approaching from the other side of the rise. A battered pickup truck bounced down the old dirt road. White dust spun off the rear tires, billowing out behind it like a parachute, as the old truck pulled up to my Aunt Lydia's house. The sun shone yellow amid a high California sky. All the dust floated up and out toward the sun. For a moment, I thought the truck might dissipate in a cloud of dust, a thick cough of exhaust spreading up and away, thinning into nothing.

What happened was something more surprising than that, though.

Two white men in their late forties climbed out of the truck, their legs stiff and bowlegged from many hours of riding. The shorter man craned his neck to look back at the road while the taller man checked something he'd written down in a spiral-bound notepad.

Kenny tapped me gently on the shoulder and we walked out toward the truck. I put my feet into my unlaced boots and re-clasped the belt on my old jeans before we hit the porch. I looked out through the partly open screen door. Kenny peeked out from behind my elbow.

"Are you lost?" I asked.

The smaller of the two, wearing jeans and cowboy boots, slunk back toward the truck, but the other man smiled and tipped his cap, a blue Kansas City Athletics baseball cap that had faded long ago.

"Does Ernest Walker live near here?" he asked.

"Not anymore," I said.

Ernest Walker had been a field hand at the Hudson Farm. He had lived in a shack about two miles down the road, back in among the trees. Kenny had led me to the place about a week after we arrived in the County. Walker had been a blues musician. Kenny really dug that sort of thing. The Blues. I did, too. A little bit, anyway, although I didn't like to admit it. I was into the street corner sounds of doo-wop. I liked the way the girls faces would light up when I'd come in with that big bass voice of mine when we covered songs by the Dells or The Spaniels. Blues was an older form of music, rustic, uncouth, and not as popular with the ladies, particularly the young ones. Even then, I knew Kenny was going to make us famous. He sang all of Frankie Lyman's songs and the covers we did of the Cadillacs and El Doradoes. But we'd played around a couple of times with Walker. Mostly I'd been humoring Kenny. Walker wasn't around anymore though, not for about a month.

"Used to," I said, trying to say it so

they'd understand. "He's down at Mendal House."

The taller man started to ask directions.

"It's the colored hospital," I told him. The way I said it, I hoped I'd made it clear. Ernest Walker had a better shot at surviving a life sentence at San Quentin Penitentiary than ever returning from where he was now.

"Can you take us? We've come a long way. We could pay you."

Before I could reply, the shorter man nudged his companion and pointed behind me.

At the mention of Walker, Kenny had pushed his way out under my arm and onto the porch. Butterflies had come to him, fluttering cascades of yellow and white and blue.

"How about that," the shorter man said, dumbfounded. I looked at Kenny. He stared intensely at me. He nodded imperceptibly. He wanted to see Walker again. At least that's what I made of his stare. I looked back at the tall man. "All right," I said, "we'll show you the way."

So much for driving a hard bargain. But I didn't feel like I had much choice. And the butterflies, still arriving in larger numbers, were starting to unnerve me anyway. It was time to move.

"The guitars," Kenny said calmly. "We'll need to get Walker's guitars." They must have been the first words he'd spoken in days.

Both men looked surprised, like they thought Kenny couldn't talk, or maybe just that this black kid sounded as if he'd come out of some sort of snooty, big city prep school. The short man didn't seem too pleased with the whole business, but the other man smiled and held out his hand. His name, he told us, was Milo Johnson. His friend was Aaron Silvers. Kenny, a swirl of butterflies in his wake, jumped into the back of the truck.

"Further down the road," I told Mr. Johnson, "that's where Walker lived."

"O.K.," he said, motioning Mr. Silvers into the bed of the pickup. "Let's go."

I pushed through eddies of wings and shadow-flickering light. The butterflies happened to Kenny a lot, during summer months.

"What's with that?" I asked Kenny once.

"Souls," he said, "broken, incomplete, waiting for their return."

I didn't understand and didn't push it. I just ignored it, like so much about my brother.

I climbed in the cab of the truck so that I could give directions. Silvers rode in the back with Kenny. They had equipment under tarps in the back, electronic stuff of some kind. Kenny looked a little sick. It was hard to relax in the back of the pickup. The wind whipped across his face as the truck bounced up and down on the dirt road. Mr. Silvers didn't look comfortable, either. His outside hand held a rigid death grip on the edge of the truck. At least we quickly left the butterflies far behind.

The Hudson farm, as far as I knew, didn't have any other field hands besides

Walker. During harvest season, migrant farm workers were brought in by the dozens in old, dilapidated school buses.

Sand and scrub gave way all at once to sweeps of irrigated green fields as we neared the farm.

We drove down winding paths that made the dirt road we'd come down earlier seem like a superhighway. Finally we turned off-road past a line of trees, pulling up just fifty yards later in front of a tiny shack at the edge of a small field.

We piled out of the truck, and the two men exchanged silent looks. Kenny pushed the shack's door open and peered inside.

An elderly white woman in a wood-paneled truck pulled in behind us. Mrs. Hudson was tall and upright, her back stiff as a washboard as she walked up to us. Her two dogs growled softly at us from where they were tied down in the back of the pickup truck. A pair of rifles lay across the rack in the back window.

She scowled and walked past me to talk to our companions.

"What do you want with these two?" she asked.

Mr. Silvers began to stammer a reply.

"It better not be something dirty." A pair of black teenagers accompanied by two middle aged white men wasn't an everyday occurrence in Morgan Creek. We were a long way, both spiritually and in miles, from San Francisco.

"We're looking for Ernest Walker," Mr. Johnson said. He kept his voice soft, but there was a slight strain in his speech that I wouldn't have noticed if we hadn't talked earlier. "These two boys were kind enough to help. They said he lived here."

"He's not here."

"They're going to show us the way to Mendal House."

Kenny walked out with two guitars in his hands and a shoebox under his arm that I knew had Walker's photographs, some of them decades old.

"You going to take his stuff to him?" Mrs. Hudson asked. "I need to clean out his room."

"He'd want these," Kenny said to me.

"We're taking him everything that matters," I told Mrs. Hudson.

"Well, you just be sure to get those things to him," she snapped.

We drove away without looking back.

M ENDAL HOUSE STOOD BETWEEN a pair of vacant lots on the corner of Second Avenue and Pine Street, in what passed for downtown in Morgan Creek. I'd never been inside before. The ancient wood-frame structure had been built over 100 years ago, back when the train had carried miners north to gold rush territory. It was easy to see your future in the weathered building. I had an uncle who had died there. Someday, if I stayed close to home, I would too. I wasn't going to stay close.

The nurse on duty wasn't going to let us in at all, but Mr. Johnson told her he worked for a record company looking to tape some of the great old bluesman before they died. Walker was one of the ones they had tracked down. It had taken them months. Mr. Johnson also paid out some money. So the equipment in the back of the truck was recording equipment. Kenny and I carried the guitars and the shoebox.

We found Walker in a closed in room at the back of the building. He looked emaciated and he had dark splotches on his face I hadn't seen before. His hair had turned all gray from the salt-and-pepper of just a couple of months ago. His sad brown eyes had sunk even further into his head. Walker had on a dirty white gown open at the back. He had trouble breathing; Kenny had to help him to a sitting position on the bed. He had nothing in his room besides his bed and a bedstand, not even a roommate. The other bed sat empty, unmade except for a single white sheet. The floors were made of cracked tile, green flecked with white and black. The walls had spiderwebs in the plaster and his one window wouldn't open anymore. Mr. Johnson and Mr. Silvers introduced themselves. Walker nodded at them, but smiled at Kenny. He took the shoebox, and we all sat quietly while Kenny and Walker looked at the pictures. He named places in the pictures that he had played twenty, thirty, fifty years before.

Eventually, Walker had Kenny get the guitars and sit by him. The two began to play. Mr. Silvers started the machine they'd brought, which hissed softly as it turned. Walker had to stop to stretch his fingers. He had arthritis. But he played on. This might be his last performance. He and Kenny traded some licks.

Walker's voice, when he began to sing, sounded badly worn. Mr. Silvers brought him a glass of water from a tap in the backroom and after that Walker's voice filled out. The rasping quality was still there, but now it sounded as if it came from experience, from too many nights spent away from home, playing in bars and nightclubs, drinking whiskey. Sometimes he broke from singing to make jokes or tell a story. It was sad and great and full.

I wanted to be him so bad right then. It was my curse, of course, to always want the limelight and never be able to step into it myself. It was waiting for Kenny.

They stopped when Mr. Silvers ran out of tape.

"Just a minute," he said, "and you can start up again."

Kenny had been accompanying Walker, playing a steady rhythm while Walker showed off his skills on the guitar. But as they started up again Kenny became more assertive in his playing. And when they started up in to "Diving Duck Blues," Kenny took the vocals.

> If the river was whiskey, Mama,
> Then I was a diving duck.
> I would dive to the bottom.
> Lord, I'd never come up.

I was startled that Kenny would cut in on Walker's session like that. But more shocking still was the way he sang. Kenny's high, youthful voice had terrific range.

But as he sang now his voice sounded modulated, like an older man singing falsetto. It was chilling in the same way as a performance by Peetie Wheatstraw or Skip James could be, two musicians who were rumored, along with Robert Johnson, to have sold their souls to the devil in exchange for their blues talents.

Walker turned his head and looked for a while at Kenny, just stared into his face, the veins of his neck twisting beneath the loose skin as he leaned forward. Then, apparently reassured, he leaned back and strummed a few notes as he tuned his guitar.

He started to sing a song I'd never heard before. More of a chant than a blues tune. His guitar playing was soft, yet piercing, as he used a bottle neck to bend the high notes.

Two angels came from heaven
    And rolled my stone away
The lord'll bear my spirit home
    After I've passed my time away

If I had wings like a dove
　　　　I would fly
But I was born to die
　　　　And lay this body down
When my trembling spirit flies
　　　　Unto a world unknown

His rage clearly simmering, Walker stared defiantly at Kenny the whole way through the song. The mood of the recording session had unraveled completely.

When he finished at last, Kenny stood up, pushing his chair away.

"If that's the way you feel old man," he said. "I'll go. I thought you'd be happy to see me again." And with the guitar still in his hands, he walked out.

Horrified, I started to apologize, to Walker, to everybody, when I heard an engine turn over and the pickup truck we'd ridden in earlier pull away. By the time I reached the front door, there was no sign of Kenny or the truck.

MR. JOHNSON OWNED THE TRUCK Kenny drove off in. Luckily, Mr. Silvers was able to rent a beat up, blue four-door Chevy Impala from a nearby auto shop. It took the better part of an hour to find the car and finish haggling with the shop's owner. Mr. Johnson, Mr. Silvers and I searched all over town for Kenny with no luck. I had them drive me out to a few places that I thought Kenny might have gone to simmer down, but the evening wind kicking up and the setting sun forced me home to tell Aunt Lydia.

When I arrived, she was in the kitchen cooking up some food, just beans and rice with Creole spices. My mouth watered. Aunt Lydia was a nurse in the hospital the next town over, and was gone from first light to last. She always told us she didn't have time to cook for us and clean for us and we had to make do-and we did all right for ourselves-but she always tried to take care of us like Momma would, leaving us rice and sausages wrapped up in paper in the icebox, or wiping Kenny's dirty face with the corner of a wet cloth. She had taken us in for the summer as a favor to Momma, and I hated to have to tell her Kenny had run off. She didn't need more worries.

Aunt Lydia had changed out of her nurse's uniform into a light summer dress, orange and white, a dress from some other time in her life than now. Some other place than her lonely house. She had absent-mindedly left her hair up in a nurse's tight, efficient bun. Sweat stuck the dress to her back as she stirred over the hot stove. I let the screen door slam as I stepped in to the smell of Louisiana spices, my stomach constricting with fear and hunger both. She hummed, turning to me, stopping when she saw my face.

I told her everything, my lower lip trembling. Well, I didn't tell her everything—I told her about meeting Mr. Johnson and Mr. Silvers and going to Mendal House and Kenny playing with Old Man Walker and that Kenny had gotten mad, left and driven off before anyone could stop him. I left out the part about the strange voice Kenny used and what passed between Kenny and Walker. I couldn't explain that anyway, not even to myself.

Aunt Lydia hugged me hard. She cried, but had a look on her face like she'd seen herself through things before. She only said, "Kenny," once, sadly, and "what will I tell Kat?" Kathleen. Her sister. My mother. Kenny's and mine. When Aunt Lydia went outside to talk to Mr. Johnson and Mr. Silvers, I ate my fill of rice and beans. I was hungry, but I couldn't taste a thing.

O**N THE PHONE THAT FIRST** night we lost Kenny, Momma had been hysterical but then preternaturally calm. "You find him," she said in a voice I'd never heard her use before. "I'm counting on you." After that, I would have walked into hell itself. Almost did, as it turned out. "I'll be on the next bus out," she said, "but you've got to do for him until then."

Momma didn't arrive until almost a full week later. By then, it was all over anyway.

T HE POLICE FOUND MR. JOHNSON's pickup two days later, parked in a ditch just outside of Munsonville, a small town fifty miles down the road. The passenger side window had been broken out and a headlight busted, a small trickle of blood across the dashboard, just enough blood to set the police looking for Kenny, even if he was just a colored runaway. But that lasted only about a day. They'd stopped looking for him by the time I rode out with Mr. Johnson and Mr. Silvers in the Impala to pick up the truck.

I planned to head into Munsonville and find Kenny myself. Aunt Lydia wanted to forbid me to go, not wanting to lose both of us, but I was getting too old to stop that way. Mr. Johnson and Mr. Silvers had driven me all around the County looking for Kenny the first few days. They felt bad, especially Mr. Johnson, but it wasn't their fault and eventually they had to move on. Mr. Johnson had offered to take me into Munsonville and get me situated before he left.

I waited in the cold while Mr. Johnson stepped into the cab of the pickup, tried the ignition, and gave a small wave back to Mr. Silvers when the truck started up. Mr. Silvers drove off before I had even climbed in beside Mr. Johnson.

Before leaving Morgan Creek, I'd visited Mendal House a few times to see if Kenny had returned there to finish whatever it was that had started between him and Ernest Walker. It was as good as any lead I had, but it didn't seem like Kenny had been there. Walker was asleep mostly when I saw him, but one time I found him awake. He lay rigid, seemingly smaller than before, like he was shrinking away. His face was slack, his mouth open and dry, lips cracked and crusted. His eyes were glazed, as if his vision was fixed on something that hovered in the middle of the room. He didn't notice me at first. His breathing labored and seemed to take all his concentration. It was like he was listening to something intently, trying to hear distant music. Finally, he seemed to notice me and looked up suddenly.

He said something I couldn't quite make out and motioned for water. I filled his half-empty glass in the back room and handed it to him. He sipped loudly, his hand shaking.

"I never did like him all that much," he said.

"Kenny?"

"No. The other one. He snored. Kept me awake nights. I was glad to see him go."

"Have you seen Kenny?" I asked, although I knew it was hopeless. Walker was going downhill fast. But the nurses hadn't seen Kenny either so he must not have come back.

"I'm sorry," Walker said, though whether to the ceiling, to me, or somebody else, I couldn't tell.

Before Mr. Johnson and I had driven

half a mile toward Munsonville, it began
to sprinkle and then to snow. Big fat white
flakes that melted before they hit the
ground. Snow in California may not be as
rare as a cold day in hell, but it's close. I felt
cursed, like I carried a mark of shame, like
there was something I should have done
for Kenny to have stopped him, stopped
everything from happening. But all I could
do about it was pull my coat in tighter
around my neck and blow ineffectually on
my hands, trying to feel something. And I
had to admit-the snow was beautiful. Cold
as death, but beautiful.

THE IMPALA HAD HAD A GOOD
heater, I missed it as the wind
whistled softly through the broken window
of the truck. Munsonville turned out
to be just lonely buildings scattered at
a crossroads. The north-south road ran
long and straight before curving around
a hillside. The east-west road didn't look
like it went anywhere, though I knew it

ran straight into the ocean in one direction and deep into impenetrable mountains in the other. Munsonville was the kind of dilapidated backwater my father used to tell me about as a child when he told me anything about growing up in Louisiana. In my father's stories it was at crossroads like this that people would come to sell their souls to the devil in exchange for a better life.

At first I thought finding Kenny was going to prove ridiculously easy after all. Munsonville seemed so small that you could walk across it from one side to the other in minutes. A motel, a decrepit movie house, a grocery store, and a saloon made up the main drag.

I checked the grocery store first and then the movie house. I wasn't allowed into the saloon, but Mr. Johnson checked it and found it empty. Next I paid for a room in the motel, a large boarding house really, owned by a freckle-faced, dark skinned woman, Mrs. Gunnerstand. If she had any reservations about renting a room to black youth without any baggage of any kind, she didn't show it. Maybe it helped that Mr. Johnson waited until I got the room before he left.

"Maybe I should stay," he said after I got the key.

"No, go on. It's not your problem," I told him.

He bit his lip, wanting to leave, I could tell, but wanting everything to be all right, too.

"You sure you're all right?"

"No. But I'm sure you can't do anything more about it that I couldn't do myself."

He nodded and looked at his feet.

"Aaron and I are going to do some more recording not too far from here tomorrow. I'll be back to find you after that, here or in Morgan Creek. If-when everything works out. Maybe we'll get on with that recording with Walker. A couple of those tracks were really special."

He shook my hand, then left, looking back more than once.

I started canvassing the streets the

next morning. Unfortunately, Munsonville turned out to be larger than it looked at first, parts of it hidden behind hills or veiled by dark copses of trees. I lost myself walking down long, winding streets that led nowhere. I no longer knew what I was looking for. Did I really expect Kenny to appear in the middle of a cow pasture or the porch of farm workers?

I found my way back to the motel for lunch. Mrs. Gunnerstand made me a big lunch and I started out again. I had tried to ask Mrs. Gunnerstand if there had been anyone new in town, a kid, but like the few other people I met, she didn't want to talk. This time I set out toward a part of town I'd previously overlooked, with its vast stretches of farmland separated by shacks and barns. It wasn't as cold as it had been the day before, but as the day waned the cold crept through me and into my bones. Where would I go next if I couldn't find Kenny, I wondered? On to the next town, perhaps. And after that? Would I have to make the long trek back home empty handed? I thought I might rather die of cold.

I was at the lowest point I'd been since Kenny had run away when I thought I heard the faint sound of a guitar. It sounded like a rhythm line, a faint echo of a train engine. Following the sound, I cut through a yard and crept between houses and came out behind a rustic shack that must have been a speakeasy before prohibition. The still was set up inside a barnyard door, in full view.

Inside the woodsy, redwood-paneled house, a small figure sat hunched over a harmonica performing before a few solitary customers seated at a few tiny tables. There was one man dancing, swaying, with his right arm bent over an imaginary partner, even though the music wasn't something you could dance to easily.

I knew at once that the harmonica player wasn't Kenny. The hands that folded over the tiny instrument were much too big.

By the time I got to the doorway I

spotted Kenny seated behind the other player, guitar in hand.

He looked older. Older than me. His face was drawn, almost gaunt. Gone were the soft lines of childhood. Even his eyes seemed smaller and his eyelids drooped as if he was ready to nod off at any moment.

He looked up at me as I entered but there was no recognition in his jaded stare.

Something felt wrong. It was cold in here. Almost like a meat locker. Colder even that it was outside.

The cold seemed to be inside me, starting in my lower back and shivering up my spine. It was darker in here then outside, too. Even with a few bare electric bulbs dangling from the ceiling. The sun was setting, so the sky outside had faded to a deep twilight, a mix of blue still behind the black, but in here it was night. The shadows seemed to push out from the corners and claim the room. What the hell was going on? I sat at one of the tables, leaning over it nervously, unwilling to leave without Kenny but unnerved, unsure how to talk to him.

Then I noticed the man dancing again. Tears ran slowly down his cheeks and he smiled, a big happy smile. "Maggie," he whispered, sobbing, "Maggie, Maggie." Around the room the other customers sat rapt, looking into corners or at wisps of smoke like they all saw something, each something different. I wanted to grab Kenny and run out of there as quickly as possible, before something I couldn't see came after me. But I knew it wasn't going to be that easy.

When the players finished their set and Kenny made his way to the kitchen, presumably to ask for food, I followed in case he decided to leave through a side door. I wasn't going to lose him now.

He slipped around a corner. When I followed I felt something hit me from behind, then an arm gripped tightly around my throat and the sharp stab of a knife blade.

"Who are you?" Kenny hissed. The tip of large kitchen knife rested against the bottom of my chin, pressing upward into the soft flesh.

"Lamond," I croaked. "Your brother." He swung me around violently to face him, keeping the knife between us. He looked me up and down.

"Sit down," he said, pointing to a back room with a dark-stained table and chairs.

"I'd rather we left this place," I said.

He shrugged.

"It's cold outside. This will do. No one will bother us."

There were people working in the kitchen, but they wouldn't look at us. And I could feel it, too, what they felt. Like they had done something wrong. Like something was wrong and they didn't want anyone to know, so no one moved or looked at each other but just did their work and hoped the feeling would let them be-the fear of being caught, found out somehow, I don't know by what. But whatever it was, Kenny somehow was, or somehow embodied, that thing that they feared.

He walked behind me, still carrying

the knife, as we made our way to the back room.

He put the knife down on the table and pulled a chair out to sit down. His guard down, I felt the urge to ... do what? Push by him and run out the door. Escape? Or try to overpower him before he could pick up the knife. And then what? Drag him home?

I sat down on the other side of the table.

"Say what you got to say," Kenny prompted. He was hunched over with his chin resting on his arms which were crossed across the table.

"I came to bring you home," I said.

"Home?" He spat. "What makes you think I want to go home?"

"We miss you."

"Who?"

"Me. Aunt Lydia. Mom's worried sick."

"Man, don't you listen, I don't know you. I'm not your brother. My name's Jones."

"Jones?"

"Emanuel Jones."

I shook my head. Nothing made any sense.

"Never heard of me, have you?"

I shook my head dumbly.

"You'd have to be about ten years older. I'd been in Mendal House almost that long, unable to play." He looked at his hands and they twitched slightly, playing imaginary strings and frets.

He smiled. A quick, darting smile, a smile meant for a guitar but not for me. He seemed fascinated by the way his hands moved.

"You're dead, aren't you?"

"You're not as stupid as you look, but you still bug the shit out of me."

"You've got to let Kenny go." I put my hand out to plead, but Kenny pushed away from the table, out of reach like I was attacking him.

"I didn't have anything to do with this. I was fine, more than fine, where I was. Starting over as a snot-nose kid isn't my idea. They laughed at me here, until I started playing. And I can't smoke; I hacked out a lung trying. And don't start me on women. Shit, I did all this already, and I don't want it. Not anymore. I'm tired."

"What are you going to do?" I said miserably.

"I don't know, but you see what happens wherever I go. Weird shit, people seeing the dead come back to life. And the cold. I can never get warm. It gets worse when I play. But that's the only thing I know how to do."

"You need to come back with me," I said firmly, mustering as much resolve into my voice as I could. "You've got nowhere else to go, am I right? And I know Kenny, maybe we can find a way to bring him back."

I didn't have a plan just then. My family was from Louisiana, maybe somebody knew some kind of voodoo thing I'd never heard about. There were rumors about some of my family practicing, in older days. No one I had ever met. That's how everyone explained Kenny—"runs in the family," they'd say, whenever something strange happened. But it didn't seem very plausible, not even to me then, but it was all I had to hold on to.

Kenny thought, rubbing his chin, years he didn't have registering in the weary look he gave me.

"All right, he said. "But keep your Mom and Aunt away from me. I don't think I could take it. I'm too old to be anybody's child."

We left through the back.

Out front, the man who had been shadow dancing was sitting in the middle of the road, his head in his hands, crying like he'd lost everything all over again. I think he had. We walked on in silence. Every shadow I saw had teeth.

A FARMER GAVE US A RIDE BACK toward Morgan Creek the next morning, early. It was windy but at least the sun had come out again, though distant and with little heat. Kenny sat tuning his guitar while we drove, but I didn't want him to play.

"Don't play," I shouted to him above the wind. "Wait."

"I didn't ask for any of this," Kenny said.

He scrunched his mouth up like a sour old man.

"I think maybe I know a way out, though," he said, with a sly grin.

"What's that?"

"I should be dead. Maybe I should just go back."

"What do you mean?" I didn't like the way his eyes seemed to recede into some distant place.

"I could just throw myself over the edge and just die."

The road unrolled below us fast. He moved to rise but I jumped on top of him, holding him down.

"Kenny," I shouted.

"I'm not Kenny," he hissed.

"Don't do it."

"You're right," he said, his body relaxing under mine, smirking at me. "You're right. I'm younger than I remember. I'd probably live. Just hurt a lot."

The farmer had glanced back when we knocked around, and now his truck rolled to a stop.

"Get out," he said. "I don't need fighting back there."

I let Kenny up and we climbed out.

The farmer looked more rattled than he should just from having a couple of boys rolling around in back. What had he seen when Kenny played?

Kenny sneered at me as the truck rattled away.

"Day was, when I could have kicked your ass."

"We'll get another ride," I said.

"Sure," Kenny said, "or, if a car goes by too fast I can just leap in front and end this farce."

"Shut up," I said. I wanted to hit him, hard in the face. If only it wasn't my brother's face, already twisted into a parody of itself.

Kenny laughed at me and shook his head until we got another ride back to Morgan Creek in the back of another empty farmer's truck.

Kenny started to play and sing. And I didn't have any heart left to stop him. At least he wasn't trying to die while he was singing. He sang a song I'd never heard before.

> I no longer know my home
> > No longer know my home
> Like one on a lonely road
> > Walks in fear and dread
> And having once turned round
> > Turns no more his head
> 'Cause he knows a frightful fiend
> > Close behind him treads.

Only when I knocked at the truck's rear window and asked the driver if he could make up some time for us, and he sped up, did Kenny stop singing.

OUR LAST RIDE INTO TOWN WAS IN a hearse, making its end run back to the funeral home from the cemetery.

We rode in the now coffinless rear with our legs stretched out. It was almost impossible to make out the landscape through the darkened windows as we traveled. I could just see the dark shapes as they passed, but they proved too elusive, too far away.

We stretched gratefully as we climbed out of the back. The sun had just begun to climb over the horizon, lighting the small town like the set of a Western movie. The houses seemed incredibly clean and insubstantial in the bright, pale sunshine.

Kenny dusted off his jeans and looked around.

"It's all different," he said.

"How do you mean," I asked. I was too tired to care, but I wanted to let him talk. I was afraid if I tried to lead him away that he wouldn't follow.

"I don't mean the mortuary. I wouldn't remember that. But these buildings. And the cars are so much smaller."

I nodded. It was strange to hear Kenny talking like an old man. He *was* an old man.

"That used to be a ballfield," he said, pointing to a row of not so old yet dilapidated buildings just down the street. "We used to have a team called the Sage."

He gazed out, something lighting up his eyes from inside.

"I guess I'm young enough to play again. Didn't think of that."

He stretched his arm back and motioned straight over his head, throwing.

"Kenny," I said. "Emanuel . . . Mr. Jones." I wasn't sure what I wanted to say.

Kenny spat, an ugly look on his face. He was starting to scare me again. His moods seem to be changing so quickly.

"We have to get back," I said. "Please. It's this way."

He turned and I led him quickly back to the hospital. We glided past the nurses—too few to really watch the door carefully. We made our way to Walker's room. He wasn't there. The beds were neatly made. The window opened to the light. His guitars sat piled in a corner, not leaning separately as a musician would leave them. Someone had just hastily put them on top of each other to get them out of the way.

"Ah, fuck," Kenny said, and sat on the bed across from Walker's.

"Mr. Walker?" I called out, not wanting to believe the obvious, as if there were somewhere for him to hide. Could he be in another room, or out somewhere?

"He's dead," Kenny said. "Sorry, kid."

I sat on Walker's bed.

We sat awhile in silence. Then Kenny started to speak without looking at me.

"This was my bed," Kenny said. "I died here."

He patted the mattress and sat down, swung his feet up and down when he realized that they didn't reach the floor.

"Walker and me," he said, "we'd known each other a long time. We had been friends, at first, a long time ago, then enemies—partly because of some things with the music—some business and some to do with, well, what we believed in—and partly, as so often happens, because of a girl. An amazing girl, I grant you. Then I'd ended up here, and Walker used to visit me sometimes, and we were, not friends, I don't know, old hands, and all the old troubles didn't matter."

Kenny shrugged and I slumped, put my hands in my pockets, not really listening. I turned away to look out the window, but Kenny, this one, went right on talking, filling the emptiness.

"And having been dead," he grinned, "I can tell you, that was right—it doesn't matter. It really doesn't. The only thing that signifies is that we had some god-damn fun before it was over."

Kenny's old voice had been flat, emotionless, but at the last he made a low moan, almost to himself. I looked at him, his eyes bore on me.

"I died here," he said. "I waited around a while. Didn't know what else to do. Thought Walker might conk out any day and then the two of us might . . . I'm not sure what. But as the days passed I felt myself fading away, forgetting who I was and everything I knew. And then I just floated away. The preacher growing up would have said that I went home to live with God. But it wasn't like that.

"It was like the universe was one big egg shell—with gigantic fissures running through it. I floated up and into a very small part of one of those cracks and healed it, made it whole. Or maybe it healed me. I can't remember anymore."

Kenny jumped off his bed and picked up the guitars. He dropped one on Walker's bed beside me and sat back on his old bed. All I could think of was butterflies, swarming in sunlight, souls, waiting. Kenny tuned his guitar, humming absently to himself.

"I thought you and Walker would play Kenny back," I said. "Like before, only in reverse."

"I know you did," Kenny said. "I got that." He motioned at the guitar beside me, but I let it lie.

Kenny began to play softly.

"Your brother's gone," he said. "If

nothing changes, I'm going to have to go soon, and make my way, playing music, I suppose. Only thing I'm any good at."

"No," I said, but I had no heart in it.

"I'm sorry, kid, I really am. I don't want his body. He can have it back. But I don't know what to do."

I heard a familiar truck outside and went to the window. Mr. Johnson, alone, without Silvers, had pulled up and stepped out of his truck. He'd said he'd come check on things. After a time filled with Kenny's expert doodling and bending of notes, Milo Johnson came into the room.

"Kenny," he said, smiling, "hey, all right. I was hoping it would work out."

I had sat back on the bed, my hands still in my pockets. I looked at him bleakly.

"It's not Kenny," I said.

Johnson stopped, even backed up to the doorway a half-step. He looked quizzically at Kenny, then at me, clearly not believing, but willing to see where this was going.

"My name is Emanuel Jones," Kenny said.

Johnson looked at Kenny for a long time, waiting for the punch line. It didn't come.

"'The Road to Calvary,'" Johnson finally said. A test.

Kenny leaned over his guitar, stretching his child's fingers to reach the chords, and began to play. He frowned deep in reverie and moaned low and guttural, eerie. I felt the hairs on the back of my neck stand up. The room itself seemed to darken as Kenny tapped his foot in time. He sang.

> Walked the road to Calvary
> > Wept beneath the cross
> But I didn't ask for this
> > I just can't bear the loss,
> > > Just can't bear the loss.

> Can't stay and say I'm sorry
> > Just can't bear the loss
> Can't stay in safe harbor
> > My soul all tempest-tossed,
> > > my soul's tempest-tossed.

Kenny croaked out the verses. In between singing he returned to his guttural humming, a sad sound of shadow-filled rooms and cigarettes and things better left unsaid. Kenny sang from old pain and sorrow. I started to cry for Kenny, for *my* Kenny. Johnson just stared with the most peculiar look on his face until Kenny finished.

Johnson started to speak, his voice failed him. He swallowed dryly.

"Stay here," he said. "I'll be back." He left to get his equipment. The nurses had come with the music, but Mr. Johnson soothed their complaints with money, explanations.

"But why can't you play somewhere else," the head nurse asked, "Can't you take these kids somewhere else to play?"

Johnson had simply handed her more money and they left us alone. Johnson quickly got a tape on the reels and got it rolling.

"Mr. Jones," he said, "please."

Kenny began to play. I fell over on

my side, lying on the bed, tears drying on my cheeks, my nose running. But I kept my hands in my pockets, not even caring enough to wipe my face while Kenny was lost somewhere. Not caring while Jones played to spite the living, come back from shadows and nothingness. I stopped listening when I felt something behind my temples, then my head throbbed painfully in time to the music. I sat up without realizing it and picked up the other guitar. No, I didn't. Or, maybe I did.

It happened so fast. I couldn't tell if it was a decision I had made or if somebody else, Walker, perhaps, had reached for my body. Anyway, I thought I could feel Walker there with me, suddenly there, his deep brown eyes and lined cheeks, sallow and care-worn, staring out from beneath my brow.

In any event, something at that point rushed at me from a long distance and shoved me out of myself completely. I tumbled away into a corner of the room and looked back at myself as I started to play.

I stood, tried to right myself, to find my bearings. But I kept slipping. Without a body, my spirit was incredibly light, buoyant.

I started to float away. The world around me seemed to cease. I stood up somewhere else, somewhere first dark, then shadowed with light and fleeting shapes. There was a signpost of decayed wood. It read "Golgonooza" and was sharpened to a point on one end. I followed the sign's direction down a dusty road shrouded in mist until I saw light ahead. A two-story building hunched at a dead-end, eaves overhanging a porch. A sign swinging from the overhang was too worn to read. The place looked like a bar, a gin joint from some earlier time. Its walls were darkly stained, the wood badly warped. I could hear the walls creaking loudly, then, getting closer, I heard voices, singing, music filtering out. I could see shapes inside behind pulled shades that glowed with a soft light. The door stood ajar.

I stepped nosily across the sagging

planks of the porch and pushed through the door. I hadn't known how cold I was until the heat of the crowded room blasted me. An enormous man in dark glasses, a thin mustache and a neatly tailored brown suit with a thin black tie on a white shirt nodded at me as I entered.

"Come freely," he said, smiling, "and leave something of what you bring."

He motioned me toward an open table at the edge of the circle of yellow light that dominated the center of the room. The room sweated with music, many people playing, bathed in that light, trading riffs or weaving their music in and around one another. The musicians huddled into the light but still more played in the blackness beyond it. It was impossible to tell how many people were there. I could see at least a half-dozen guitarists, an upright bass, two saxophones, a trumpet; somewhere in the darkness, a drum beat and the faint tinkling of piano keys. In the darkness, bright coals of cigarettes flickered and yellow light reflected off dark glasses like headlights glinting off the eyes of wolves just off the road.

Kenny sat in the inner circle, head fallen back in abandon, not looking while his fingers scratched angrily at the strings of his guitar; his fingers bled, his face scrunched up in a grimace, but he nodded to himself like everything was just right somehow.

I should get him out of here, I thought. But how? Where was I?

For a moment I did nothing. Something held me back, some bit of corrupted knowledge about magic that I could only articulate to myself by thinking: never wake a sleepwalker. I had found Kenny, and I didn't want to hurt him by disrupting whatever he was doing too quickly. But then I meant to sit down, and didn't. In confusion, I stumbled into the light.

"Please," I shouted, "Please, Kenny, please."

Kenny looked and held me for a time with his clear eyes, deep like stones in a river. And he sang a song whose words I cannot remember. I can still catch fragments, but not the tune. And not a single word. But it made me stop for a moment, all those wolves eyes glinting, all those firefly lights in the darkness. I should have held still, but I reached out and touched Kenny's hand. I thought of Mom coming, and I thought of Kenny lost. But mostly I thought of me—of how I missed and needed him, how we would play together in our band and I wouldn't end up in Mendal House; we would go—he would take me—away from a life I hated, feared. I wanted something from him so much that I reached out and touched him and broke the spell he wove.

I touched him and something seemed to drop away from him. The music kept on, a bass solo stepping in where Kenny faltered. Kenny's eyes focused, seemed to see me for the first time; then he lowered his head and stopped playing.

"Hey, Charlie," Kenny said over his shoulder to the bassist, "another live one, like us."

The serious bass player with the ragged beard and deep frown didn't stop. He looked familiar, like we'd met somewhere. But I kept my attention on Kenny.

"It's good to see you, brother," Kenny said softly, eyes still lowered from me, "but you're early."

Kenny examined his fingers, bleeding darkly.

"I didn't feel a thing," Kenny said. He pressed the tips together to staunch the flow.

"Hey, William," Kenny said, standing unsteadily, "come take my place." An old white man with a great beard stepped up. He wore a loose-fitting white shirt and hand-made coarse pants. He took the guitar and sat in Kenny's place. "I'm going outside a moment."

Kenny took my hand. The new guitarist grinned at me beatifically. He and Kenny were the only ones not wearing dark glasses. He had green eyes that blazed, glittering like supernovae. Before we got outside, weaving through tables, the man sang of the four-fold path, of angels in trees scolding him, of him scolding them back.

Then I was outside with Kenny, my head suddenly clearing in the cold.

Kenny closed the door and turned, creaking the floorboards of the porch.

"What are you doing here?" Kenny asked, without enthusiasm. He looked tired. This wasn't where he belonged. I think only the dead belonged here.

I shivered with cold sweat, and felt ill, lost, fading. The shadows seemed to be taking substance, to be closing in. I wasn't even sure that the gin joint was there anymore. Was I standing in the mist, on the road? Was there even still a road?

"I need you to come back. I promised. . . . We've got to get out of here. You need to get out of here."

I rambled. I couldn't even see Kenny clearly anymore, a fog obscuring him. But Kenny didn't let go of my hand. Still, he wouldn't look up at me.

"This is a good place," Kenny said. "Where I want to be. I'm not lost."

I panicked then. I broke down. I felt myself whirling into the shadows, my legs drifting into smoke and mist. I begged Kenny. I reached out to shake him, to make him look at me. I felt my eyes going, my vision receding as I fell into nothingness.

"Don't let go," I pleaded. "Kenny, don't let go."

I sobbed and cried hysterically and reached out madly grasping at him until I felt hands, two solid hands, holding me. And a floor solid below me. I was on my back. These were real hands and a voice

"Calm down, child, calm," over and over. The voice spoke sternly, authoritatively. I looked into the eyes of a nurse at Mendal House. I was in Walker's room.

"What are you going on about?" The nurse asked.

As I calmed, my breath slowing, I saw Kenny—I saw what looked like Kenny sitting on Jones's bed. I lay back.

"I don't need this nonsense on my watch."

Milo Johnson was handing the woman yet more money, and grabbing his equipment up as quickly as he could. The nurse hustled us out and into the street. All I could think was that the uneasy light through the clouds made the time uncertain. When was it? Then I wondered, was it Kenny who walked quietly beside me, his head bowed? The nurse had had to help me out, and I leaned heavily against the railing out front. The nurse left us there, primly telling us we were never welcome there again. I looked at Kenny but he wouldn't look at me. Even as tired as I was, I couldn't help smiling.

Milo Johnson couldn't get away fast enough. I guess it hadn't looked so good at the end there. Despite my condition, he didn't press giving us a ride. He asked, but Kenny waved him off and the truck jerked away in a cloud of dust. He had tapes of both sessions, of course, but what good were tapes of a couple of kids pretending to be dead singers? Who would want them?

We walked home with our hands in our pockets.

Aunt Lydia actually shouted out her thanks to God, testifying for almost half a minute. She fed us well and asked for stories, touching Kenny's cheek again and again until he shook her off. Kenny wouldn't speak. I told her things about where I traveled, but nothing of the land of shadows. She could tell—who wouldn't have?—that my story was incomplete, but she was too happy, and relieved, to press it. Momma would arrive the next day. Kenny, still not speaking, accepted Aunt Lydia's caresses and fussing a little longer, then yawned a few times and headed to bed.

I followed him.

We brushed our teeth and climbed into our narrow beds in a daze. I pulled the blankets over me, grateful to feel them against my skin, grateful to feel anything. I could feel a knot of terror in me, a knot I would never really lose, about the emptiness of the shadows in the place where I found Kenny.

I sat up suddenly.

"Kenny?" I asked. "Is it you? You haven't said a word. You're not Jones?"

The blanket fell around me. Kenny

had his back turned to me. He didn't move except to sigh. He spoke in a tired voice, defeated and small, a whisper.

"It's me," he said. "I'm here."

"It was terrible there," I said. "Sad."

"No," I could barely hear him say, "it wasn't."

Though I looked at him for a long time, Kenny didn't speak further. Eventually I lay back, thinking about what he had lost. We would start our band, singing soul first, then funk, making hits. Kenny would always be distracted, looking for something. People would come to hear him sing of outer space and a future that would bring all us aliens together into One. They would call him Prophet and seek him out, even follow him. Only I would know what Kenny really lost, the true geography of his outer space, his fantasies of dream worlds where the lost chord played. Only I knew the land of the shadows.

I would be Kenny's manager, my brother's keeper, building his career, our career. My eyes on the money he never cared about, on the airplay, on the fame. He would never be right, whole, again, from that day to this. But I couldn't change a thing and, to my shame, though I love him, I knew I wouldn't change things even if I could. The sets he played were like revival meetings, séances, gospel singing, all in one. He set people free, out of his loss. They needed him. I needed him.

I could see all this, our future gigs, the people coming to touch him, desperate as I had been desperate in that other place. I could see it all that night, sense it before us. I heard it in Kenny's "I'm here," spoken forlornly.

I wanted it all too much to be sorry, but I am sorry. I slept only after a long, uncomfortable, hot time of tossing, turning. My dreams were shadows, swirling.

Next day Momma arrived on the bus. She wore her traveling dress, dark blue and serious, and a frown at first. Then there were smiles and hugs and "let me look at you." Kenny got most, but I was not left out. Kenny surprised me by speaking up and telling his story. Everything. Momma and Aunt Lydia listened pensively, with pursed lips. When Kenny finished, Momma sighed.

"It runs in the family," she said.

And that was about it.

Momma and Aunt Lydia traded gossip about the family and cooked up more food than we could eat. And later, Momma made Kenny tell her everything again, as we sat sipping lemonade in the sun.

Then she said, "take it easy, will you, for a while?" to Kenny while touching his cheek.

"I will, Momma," he said, butterflies circling him with friendly waves.

"And you," she said to me, "take care of him. He needs you."

And I hoped he did. I wanted him to badly, but I doubted it—a doubt I kept tight and darkly bundled with my shame and my knotted fear in a place somewhere in my gut. I would never lose any of them, ever.

"I will, Momma," I said.

People eat up Kenny's stories about being from somewhere behind the sun, dancing with aliens from Groove. Sometimes I think he believes it, too, somehow. But I know this isn't science fiction but some kind of ghost story. And I hear it in the music. I hear it in the beat and in his chanting growls late into the night that bring the audience to some ecstasy of sweet dreaming and patchouli oil, through marijuana and the beat, to dancing and the One. But there's more than joy there, as my brother preaches. There's terror, too, a nothingness. I know that.

I know it, even if he doesn't.

ABOUT THE AUTHORS

DAVID SANDNER is a member of SFWA and the HWA. His work has appeared in *Asimov's*, *Weird Tales*, *Realms of Fantasy*, *Pulphouse*, *Mythic Delirium*, and anthologies *Baseball Fantastic*, *The Mammoth Book of Black Magic*, and *Tails of Wonder and Imagination*. He is the author of *The Fantastic Sublime* and Mythopoeic Award-nominated *Critical Discourses of the Fantastic, 1712-1831*, and editor of *Fantastic Literature: A Critical Reader*, *The Treasury of the Fantastic* (with Jacob Weisman), and *Philip K. Dick: Essays of the Here and Now*. He is a Professor of Romanticism and Popular Literature at California State University, Fullerton.

JACOB WEISMAN is the publisher at Tachyon Publications, which he founded in 1995. He is a World Fantasy Award winner for the anthology *The New Voices of Fantasy*, which he co-edited with Peter S. Beagle, and is the series editor of Tachyon's critically acclaimed novella line, including the Hugo Award–winning *The Emperor's Soul*, by Brandon Sanderson, and the Nebula and Shirley Jackson award–winning *We Are All Completely Fine*, by Daryl Gregory. His writing has appeared in *The Nation*, *Realms of Fantasy*, the *Louisville Courier-Journal*, *The Seattle Weekly*, and *The Cooper Point Journal*.

Photo © 2018 by Michael Arnzen

OTHER TITLES IN THE
NOVELETTE SERIES
from Fairwood Press:

Mingus Fingers
by David Sandner & Jacob Weisman
small paperback: $8.00
ISBN: 978-1-933846-87-3

The Archronology of Love
by Caroline M. Yoachim
small paperback: $6.00
ISBN: 978-1-933846-96-5

The Specific Gravity of Grief
by Jay Lake
small paperback: $8.99
ISBN: 978-1-933846-57-6

Welcome to Hell
by Tom Piccirilli
small paperback: $8.00
ISBN: 978-1-933846-83-5

If Dragon's Mass Eve Be Cold and Clear
by Ken Scholes
small paperback: $8.99
ISBN: 978-1-933846-86-6

Slightly Ruby
by Patrick Swenson
small paperback: $8.00
ISBN: 978-1-933846-64-4